ELLYSE PERRY

─✢─────────────✢─

POCKET ROCKET

A Random House book
Published by Penguin Random House Australia Pty Ltd
Level 3, 100 Pacific Highway, North Sydney NSW 2060
www.penguin.com.au

First published by Random House Australia in 2016

Copyright © Penguin Random House Australia 2016

The moral right of the author and the illustrator has been asserted.

All rights reserved. No part of this book may be reproduced or transmitted by any person or entity, including internet search engines or retailers, in any form or by any means, electronic or mechanical, including photocopying (except under the statutory exceptions provisions of the Australian *Copyright Act 1968*), recording, scanning or by any information storage and retrieval system without the prior written permission of Penguin Random House Australia.

Addresses for the Penguin Random House group of companies can be found at global.penguinrandomhouse.com/offices.

National Library of Australia
Cataloguing-in-Publication entry

Creator: Clark, Sherryl, author
Title: Pocket rocket / Sherryl Clark, Ellyse Perry
ISBN: 978 0 14378 124 0 (pbk)
Series: Ellyse Perry; 1
Target audience: For primary school age
Subjects: Girls – Juvenile fiction
         Cricket stories
         High schools – Juvenile fiction
Other creators/contributors: Perry, Ellyse, author
Dewey number: A823.3

Cover photograph of Ellyse Perry by Steven Chee/DLM Australia
Cover and internal illustration by Jeremy Lord
Cover design by Hannah Janzen
Internal design and typesetting by Midland Typesetters, Australia
Printed in Australia by Griffin Press, an accredited ISO AS/NZS 14001:2004
Environmental Management System printer

Penguin Random House Australia uses papers that are natural, renewable and recyclable products and made from wood grown in sustainable forests. The logging and manufacturing processes are expected to conform to the environmental regulations of the country of origin.

SHERRYL CLARK WITH

ELLYSE PERRY

POCKET ROCKET

ILLUSTRATIONS BY
JEREMY LORD

RANDOM HOUSE AUSTRALIA

CHAPTER ONE

As they drew closer, Ellyse felt her heart do a little skip. Callinan Girls' College looked amazing! With its curved walls and leafy trees, sports grounds and old red-brick buildings, it was a world away from her old school.

Ellyse's dad looked over at her and grinned. 'Ready for high school?' he asked.

'I guess so. I just wish . . .' *I just wish I'd grown a bit*. Ellyse had been one of the smallest in her Year Six class. She'd hoped to grow over the summer but it hadn't happened.

'You'll be fine,' he said. He pulled into the school drop-off zone and she opened her door. 'Knock 'em for six, kid.'

Ellyse waved goodbye and headed for the gate, running her fingers along the high brick wall that was already sun-warm to the touch.

'Hey, boofhead, you going to play frisbee with that hat?' said a familiar voice.

Ellyse whirled around to face Jamie, her friend from primary school. He was all dressed up in a neatly ironed, brand-new uniform, just like her. Except his was for the boys' school up the road.

She pulled her round hat low over her eyes. 'Boofhead yourself. Where's your gross purple cap?'

Jamie made a face. 'I forgot it. That'll be detention on the first day, I bet.' Jamie was always forgetting things – everything but his sports gear. 'It's going to be weird not playing cricket on the oval with you at lunchtime.'

Ellyse sighed. 'I know, but I'll see you after school at the park, right?'

'For sure. Better go.'

He ran off towards his school while Ellyse followed the crowd of girls that swarmed through the Callinan gates and up the drive. Everyone seemed to know where they were going. Tall girls bustled past, talking at the tops of their voices about their holidays and laughing.

Ellyse slowed and peered over the hedge. *Cool, tennis courts. But where's the cricket field?*

'Hurry up, young lady,' a voice snapped behind her.

Ellyse turned and saw a stern-looking woman with short, spiky steel-grey hair frowning down at her.

'Year Seven?' the woman asked.

Ellyse nodded.

'Into the school hall, then. The bell is about to ring.'

Ellyse followed the woman's pointing finger towards the large hall and hoisted her schoolbag higher on her shoulders. It weighed a tonne with all her new books, her laptop and lunch.

An arm circled her neck and gave her a hug, nearly toppling her over. 'Hey, isn't this awesome?'

Jazz! At last – someone I know. 'Yeah, can't wait to check out the sports teams,' Ellyse said, grinning.

'Oh, you,' Jazz replied, rolling her eyes. 'What about the drama centre and the library and the chess club?'

'Uh, no thanks,' Ellyse said. 'Did you know we could do rowing here too?'

'Yeah, and fencing.'

They made their way into the hall and found a space not too near the front. 'Where's Charlie?' Ellyse asked.

Jazz shrugged. 'Her mum's started a new job, so I think she had to catch the bus.'

Ellyse craned her neck and caught a glimpse of Charlie trying to push her way through a group of girls standing in the doorway. 'There she is.'

She waved madly until Charlie spotted her and came over, lugging a schoolbag that looked even heavier than Ellyse's. Charlie dumped it on the ground with a loud *thud*.

Before she could say hello, a bell shrilled through the hall and the stern woman began shouting at everyone to sit down and be quiet.

'Wow, she's on the warpath already,' Jazz muttered.

Charlie let out a groan. 'We'd better be in the same class.'

After a long list of rules and a speech about upholding school values, the names for each homeroom were read aloud. Ellyse held her breath. *Please let us be together. What would I do without Jazz and Charlie?*

'Class 7A,' the woman boomed, then proceeded to yell name after name.

Charlie let out a little squeak when hers was called. Jazz and Ellyse waited, hoping to hear their names too.

'Class 7B,' the stern woman announced. 'Ellyse Perry.'

'Maybe it'll be us two?' Ellyse whispered, and Jazz crossed her fingers.

But then, for 7C, they heard: 'Jasmine Theodosi.'

'I don't want to be on my own!' Jazz whined.

'Who's making all that noise?' the stern woman barked, glaring at the sea of girls. 'Right, everyone to their homerooms, thank you.'

There was a sudden uproar as sixty girls began to chatter all at once and head for the doors.

'I don't believe it,' Charlie said gloomily. 'This sucks.'

'I guess we can still spend lunchtime and recess together,' Ellyse said, but her insides felt all squishy.

Charlie flung her arms up in the air. 'Who's going to help me with maths? And lend me a pink pen when I need it?'

Jazz stopped and frowned. 'Where are the homerooms for Year Seven? Maybe we need to follow someone.'

Ellyse looked around.

An older girl smiled at them. 'Come with me, guys. I'm your guide for today.' As the girls followed her, she pointed out buildings and landmarks. 'That's the gym, that's the library, and over there is the path to the sports fields.' She grinned. 'I guess none of you play cricket. Netball, maybe?'

'I play cricket,' Ellyse said. 'We won our primary school championship last year, didn't we?'

Jazz and Charlie nodded vigorously.

'Really?' The older girl smiled again. 'I'm Nicola, and I'm on the school cricket team. We're always looking for new players.'

'That's me,' Ellyse said.

Nicola eyed her. 'You're a bit small yet, though.'

Jazz made a face at Nicola's back but Ellyse didn't bother to reply. She'd heard it so many times that she'd given up protesting. Show them on the field, her dad always told her.

'Here you are,' Nicola said. 'Rooms B42, 43 and 44. The "B" stands for Brandford Building, which is where we are. Think you can remember all that?'

The girls nodded, and Nicola went off to find other lost students. Ellyse said goodbye to her friends and entered her homeroom alone. Everyone looked as excited and nervous as she felt, and that cheered her up. Amy and Rose, two girls from her old school, waved at her.

'Find a seat, everyone.' The teacher up the front had a friendly face and was beaming at them all.

Ellyse slid into a seat in the third row. She was glad she didn't have Ms Grumpy Spikehair for homeroom.

'We don't have much time before first period,' the teacher went on, 'so let's look at your timetables and make sure you all know where to go.'

Ellyse peered down at hers. There were so many subjects she wondered how she was going to fit them all in, and every subject was in a different room. It made her miss her Year Six classroom with its walls covered in bright artwork and posters.

She scanned the list for PE. *Hmm, only two periods a week.* She'd picked two sports electives – cricket and swimming – but there was only swimming scheduled, on a Wednesday afternoon. *Where's cricket?* she thought, and scanned her timetable again. *Debating? How's that even possible? I hate speaking in front of people!* Ellyse slumped down in her chair and closed her eyes. *Charlie's right – this place sucks!*

CHAPTER TWO

The morning went by in a whirl. Recess was short, and Ellyse barely had time to eat her snack. Charlie spent the whole break complaining about how the seats were arranged alphabetically. 'So now I have to sit at the back and the maths teacher writes really, really small on the board.'

'What about you, Jazz?' Ellyse asked.

'My maths teacher looks like a lawyer,' Jazz replied. 'He wears a suit.'

Ellyse was about to have maths next – a double period. *Ugh*. Even though her dad was a maths teacher, and he made maths fun, an hour and a half of it seemed like forever. High school felt so overwhelming. *I'll never get used to it*, she thought.

Charlie insisted on borrowing her pink and purple pens, so Ellyse had to tip out her bag to find them, stressing the whole time that she'd be late to class. As she tried to sneak in the door, the teacher turned and glared. It was the lawyer! His tie was perfectly straight and his hair was gelled into a swish at the front.

'Miss Perry, I presume?'

The class broke into giggles.

'Yes, sorry, I had to . . . I mean . . .' Her face burned with embarrassment.

He smiled, and the glare turned into a twinkle. 'First days are always hard. Try not to be late again, okay?'

'I won't, sir, Mr... er...' *Oh no, I'm making it worse.*

He pointed to a name on the board. 'Mr Waugh.'

Ellyse smiled back, knowing she'd never forget his name since it was the same as one of Australia's best cricketers. She found a seat and pulled out her maths book. The first thing she would do, if lunchtime ever arrived, was find the cricket field and the nets. She'd brought her favourite cricket ball and was dying to do some bowling practice.

Mr Waugh talked a lot and then made them do a test – on the first day!

Ellyse was relieved it was all stuff she knew. *Imagine telling Dad I failed my first maths test!* she thought.

Finally, the bell rang for lunch. Outside, the air was muggy and thick, the sun beating down. She met Jazz and Charlie by the rose arches in front of Brandford.

'Let's eat and then go to the cricket nets,' Ellyse said.

Charlie groaned. 'No way I'm playing cricket when it's this hot.'

'Me, neither. Besides,' Jazz said, blushing, 'I have to go to the music room.'

Charlie peered at her suspiciously. 'What are you up to?'

'I, um, I just had music and now the teacher wants me to . . .' Jazz shrugged.

'But you don't play an instrument,' Ellyse said, confused. 'You can't count recorder in primary school.'

'Ms Polloni let us try out different things,' Jazz said. 'And I really liked the guitar, and –' She made a face. 'She thinks I can sing.'

'You? Sing?' Charlie snorted. 'I've heard you in the shower at sleepovers.'

Jazz looked hurt. 'We were being silly then,' she said, scuffing her shoe along the concrete.

Although Ellyse had also heard Jazz sing in the shower before, she figured she should support her friend. 'That's great, Jazz. I bet you've got an awesome voice.'

Charlie immediately agreed. 'I'm sorry, Jazzy, I was being mean. You go for it.'

The three girls found a shady spot under a tree and ate their lunches, comparing their classes and teachers.

'What electives did you get?' Ellyse asked. 'I put down cricket but I've been given debating instead. I hate debating.'

'I got tennis and drama,' Charlie said, chomping into her apple.

'Drama?' Ellyse and Jazz stared at Charlie.

'I can act a bit,' she mumbled.

'I guess we're all doing something new and different,' Jazz said. She nudged Ellyse. 'You might like debating.'

'Hmph, I don't think so.' Ellyse finished her sandwich and stood. 'I'm going to the cricket nets. Sure you don't want to come, Charlie?'

'No way!' Charlie lay back on the grass and closed her eyes.

Ellyse and Jazz grinned at each other and headed off in opposite directions.

* * *

Ellyse walked past the gym and swimming pool, breathing in the smell of chlorine. She wished she could dive into that cool water, but cricket was more important. As she went, she tossed her cricket ball in the air.

Beyond a row of bushy trees was the field, the pitch a long patch of brown in the middle. The nets were to the side against the fence, and half-a-dozen girls were in there, batting and bowling. She might have to wait for a turn, but it'd be great to have someone to bowl to.

As Ellyse got closer, she realised that all of the girls were much older. They were laughing and calling to each other, and she stopped under the last tree and watched. They were training seriously, the batters wearing helmets, pads and gloves. One of the bowlers was fast-medium, the other two were spinners. Their technique was good, and the pace bowler was getting the ball right at the batter's feet.

Oh no! I didn't bring my sports gear. Ellyse wanted to smack herself. In her eagerness to get to the nets, she'd forgotten that she couldn't possibly train in her daggy school uniform. She didn't even have her pads. Still, she could at least say hello and ask them about the school teams.

She summoned up the courage and set off across the grass. As she got near, the batter in the first net saw her, held up a hand to the bowler and pointed. The bowler turned around – it was the girl who'd shown them to their room, Nicola.

'Hiya, kid,' Nicola said with a wave. She used the bottom of her shirt to wipe her face. 'Bit hot for this, but it's fun. Have you come to have a go?' She frowned at Ellyse's uniform and black school shoes.

'Not really,' Ellyse said, feeling suddenly awkward. 'I don't have my gear. But I wanted to ask you about the school cricket teams and how to sign up.'

'Team – singular,' Nicola corrected her. 'It's just us. Are you a batter or a bowler?'

'Both,' Ellyse said. *Surely that's okay here?*

The batter walked over to join them, her mouth pursed. 'You're a bit young for the team, sorry. We're all Year Elevens and Twelves, and we play club competition too.'

Ellyse's stomach twisted. They clearly didn't think she'd be any good, and with no playing gear, she had no way to convince them. *Maybe I should just stick to playing with the club on Saturdays and forget about the school team. Except...* Ellyse hesitated. *I bet I could make the team if they'd give me a chance. I can't give up that easily.*

'If I came back tomorrow with my gear, could you at least let me try out?' she asked.

The batter looked doubtful, but Nicola nodded. 'Why not? We can always do with more players. You never know – we might be able to get enough together for a second team if there are others as keen as you.'

Ellyse grinned. 'That'd be great, thanks.'

She sat in the shade and watched the girls train. Nicola's bowling technique was good but she was letting her right hip lag a bit. Ellyse thought about when she'd first started playing and how Dad had said she could bowl spin really well, but it was about what felt better – and fast bowling felt better!

The other girl was skilled, but she wasn't varying her batting shots enough. She also let her bottom hand 'rule the roost', as Dad would say. Ellyse wondered whether she'd have to convince the coach as well as the whole team to let her play.

In the distance, the bell rang. Ellyse waved to Nicola and trudged off to geography. After that was Japanese.

Do they even play cricket in Japan? Ellyse sighed. *High school seems so big and confusing.*

She pushed the thought away and focused on tomorrow. It was much more important to prove she could be in the Callinan cricket team.

CHAPTER THREE

Ellyse was so tired she could barely haul her bag over her shoulders. She trudged out the gates, waved goodbye to Charlie and Jazz and climbed into her dad's car.

'How was your day?' Dad asked.

'Looooong,' she said, sliding down in her seat.

'Anything you want to share?'

She thought about whether to tell him or not. 'Um... I might not be able to play cricket for the school after all. They've only got one team and it's all the older girls.'

'You'll still have your club cricket,' he said.

'Yeah, but I wanted to be in the school team too. And guess what? I have to do debating for my elective instead of cricket!'

'Absolute torture,' Dad said, laughing. 'Just as well you're not shy.'

Ellyse grimaced. She hadn't felt shy until she started at Callinan, but everything seemed so much harder and there was so much to take in.

Dad gave her arm a squeeze. 'You'll be fine. Give it a couple of weeks to find your feet and settle in.'

She nodded and tried to push school out of her head. As they stopped at the pedestrian crossing, a bunch of boys from the other school walked past. 'There's Jamie.' She leaned out the window and waved.

He waved back and yelled, 'See you later at the cricket nets.'

Ellyse instantly felt better.

As soon as she was home, she changed her clothes and collected her gear, then headed across the street and into the park. She was the first to arrive and, within a few minutes, Jamie and some of the boys from her club cricket team had turned up.

'Are you going to play cricket for your school?' Ellyse asked Jamie.

'Yeah, for sure. They've got four teams and we already put our names down. What about you?'

'Only one team, but I'm not sure if I'll get in.'

Jamie looked at her like she was crazy.

'Why not?' he said, and swung his arm, pretending to bowl. '*Pow!* Pez bowls out the entire Callinan team in two overs. Callinan begs her to join their team.'

Ellyse laughed. 'Yeah, right.'

The late-afternoon air was still hot and sticky. They played for over an hour, taking turns to bat and bowl until everyone was red-faced and dripping with sweat. Ellyse tried to concentrate, but when she bowled, her balls kept going wide or too short. Once, the ball even flew out of her hand and straight up into the air. Batting was no better. She only made two decent hits each time she had a turn, and the bat felt like a block of concrete in her hands.

'She's lost her mojo,' Sandy jeered. 'Make her twelfth man on Saturday.'

'Shut your face,' Ellyse said. 'It's too hot, that's all.'

But inside, her stomach churned. She was supposed to try out with the school team tomorrow. *If I play like this, I'll never make Callinan's First XI.*

At dinner that night she was so quiet that even her brother, Damien, noticed. 'Bad first day?' he asked.

'No, it's just . . .' Ellyse paused. There was no way to explain it without sounding as though she were whining. 'It's fine. I'll settle in soon.'

CHAPTER FOUR

The next day, Ellyse made sure to take shorts, a T-shirt and runners as well as her ball. At the last minute she shoved her bat into her bag too, leaving the handle to stick out the top.

The morning seemed to drag, with a period of maths and then technology. It was hard to concentrate when all she wanted to do was get to the cricket field.

At lunchtime, Ellyse raced to the nets to meet the other girls.

Her hands shook as she pulled out her gear. *I hope I don't stuff this up!*

Nicola eyed Ellyse's bat. 'That's a great-looking piece of willow. You play club cricket, then?'

'Yep, Saturday mornings. But with the boys, because my club doesn't have a girls' team yet.'

'What's your batting average?'

'This year it's thirty-two.'

Nicola raised her eyebrows. 'That's pretty good. Let's go onto the field and see what you can do.'

Eight girls were already there doing some fielding practice and, as Nicola and Ellyse walked over to them, they stopped and gave Ellyse some odd looks.

She held her head high. *I can do this.*

'Everyone, this is Ellyse,' Nicola said. 'She's going to try out for the team.'

'You're kidding, right?' said a short girl with curly blonde hair. 'She's hardly big enough to carry the water bottles.'

The others laughed and Ellyse could feel her face growing hot.

'Don't speak too soon,' Nicola said. 'Ellyse, why don't you warm up and then bowl a few balls?'

Ellyse nodded and went through a quick round of stretches – she'd already done some while she was eating lunch with Jazz and Charlie – then headed to the end of the pitch with her ball.

'Emma's going to bat and the others will field, then we'll swap.' Nicola patted Ellyse's shoulder. 'Just relax and do your best. We're not expecting you to be a star.'

Good, because I don't want to be a star,

Ellyse thought. *I just want to be in the team!* She rolled her arm over a few more times, then paced out her run-in and got ready. She'd watched Emma the day before and knew some of her flaws. Ellyse took two deep breaths. Felt the ball in her hand. Focused on the batter and the line she wanted. *Go!*

She bowled a little slower at first, easing into it. Emma blocked her first ball and then hit her second solidly.

Time to test her. Ellyse bowled fast and went for a leg cutter. The ball landed almost exactly where she'd aimed and turned slightly, catching Emma by surprise. The ball zoomed past her and knocked the wicket out of the ground.

'Howzat!' Nicola shouted, and everyone except Emma clapped. 'Another one, Ellyse.'

Ellyse bowled again, this time trying for a yorker. It didn't quite go where she wanted but was close enough to force Emma back into defence. Two more balls that Emma barely managed to play, and that was an over.

'Let's see you on the bat,' Nicola said. 'Mind if I bowl to you?'

'Okay,' Ellyse said, and hurriedly put on her pads. Nicola gave her a spare helmet and Ellyse stood at the wicket. *Focus*, she reminded herself. *Keep your eye on the ball.*

As Nicola began her run-in, Ellyse kept a good grip on her bat, used the full face of it and defended, stopping the ball easily. Another ball, another defensive shot, and she started to feel more sure of herself. Nicola's next ball was faster – she'd been holding back! But it was a little short. Ellyse stepped forward and swung, sending the ball soaring to the boundary.

'Well played,' Nicola said with a grin. 'You picked that one.'

Three more balls, and Ellyse had sent one to the boundary again and two solidly into midfield. At the end of the over, the girls gathered around. Even Emma was looking impressed.

'You're terrific for your size,' the blonde girl said. 'If you grew a bit more, you'd have a place in the team.'

Nicola shook her head. 'I'd put her in the team now.'

'But it's not up to you,' a sharp voice interrupted.

Everyone turned and, even though she was surrounded by Year Twelve girls, Ellyse could see the spiky grey hair and glaring eyes.

Ms Parkes.

'I thought I left instructions for you to practise throwing and catching today,' Ms Parkes went on.

'This isn't the training session,' Nicola said. 'It's just lunchtime practice.'

'No time like the present,' Ms Parkes snapped. 'You all need to improve both skills, not waste time.'

The girls ducked their heads and muttered, 'Yes, Ms Parkes.'

'Ellyse is really good,' Nicola insisted. 'We think she –'

'She's too small. She'd look ridiculous on the field with the rest of you.' Ms Parkes sniffed. 'Besides, I would have to assess her myself and I don't have time. She can come back next year.' The teacher clapped her hands. 'Get on with it, girls. I'll see you after school.'

The team watched her walk away towards the main building.

Ellyse blinked hard and bent to take off her pads. At least the team thought she was good enough, even if nasty Ms Parkes wouldn't give her a chance. *I guess that's one good thing – I won't have Ms Parkes as a coach. That'd be a total nightmare!*

Nicola crouched down beside her. 'I'm really sorry, Ellyse.'

Emma nodded. 'Yeah, she's such a –'

'Don't diss the coach,' the blonde girl said quickly. 'Even if she's a witch.'

The girls laughed, but Ellyse couldn't muster a smile. All of a sudden, she hated Callinan. And to make things worse, this afternoon she had stupid debating!

CHAPTER FIVE

'So, are you in the team?' Charlie asked, when Ellyse met them going into Brandford.

'No.' Ellyse sighed. 'Ms Parkes is the coach and she hates me.'

Jazz linked arms with Ellyse. 'She'll be sorry when they lose all their interschool games again.'

'Again?' Ellyse looked at her in surprise. 'I thought Callinan had won the interschool competitions for the past five years.'

'Yeah, in other sports,' Jazz said. 'But not the cricket team.'

As she went into class, Ellyse kept thinking about Nicola and the other players. *Maybe I should give up on joining the team, especially if Ms Parkes is the coach. But the girls had been keen to have her . . .* Before the teacher arrived, she quickly texted Dad: *Cricket training after school. Pick me up at five?*

Ellyse sat at the back of the classroom, resting her head on her arms. She really didn't want to be there. Up the front, the teacher was writing on the board.

ESSENTIAL SKILLS FOR DEBATERS
* STYLE AND CONFIDENCE
* SPEED, TONE, CLARITY AND VOLUME
* MAKING YOUR CASE
* RESPONDING TO AND REBUTTING THE OPPOSITION'S ARGUMENTS

Ellyse groaned inwardly. *This is soooo boring.*

In the tree outside the window, a blackbird stared at her with yellow-ringed eyes, and she wished she could be in the tree with it, ready to fly away.

Her mind drifted to the cricket team. *Maybe I shouldn't go to training. Won't Ms Parkes just tell me to go away? If she does, she can't stop me from watching.*

'Hey, wake up.' A girl with a high ponytail nudged her. 'You're in our team.'

Ellyse recognised the girl from her homeroom. 'What team?' she asked, sitting up.

'Us three. We're supposed to get to know each other, and then next week we start working on our debate topic.' The girl frowned. 'Weren't you listening?'

Ellyse shook her head. 'Sorry. What's our topic?'

The other girl leaned over. 'All students should be banned from watching TV on weeknights.' She grimaced. 'Like I'm going to argue *that's* a good thing.'

'We have to,' the ponytail girl said. 'We're the affirmative. I'm Hu, by the way.'

'I'm Mia,' said the other girl. 'Are you good at debating, Ellyse?'

'No, I actually didn't pick this elective,' she said. 'I don't even know why I'm in this class.'

Mia laughed. 'Great. You'll be a real help. Not.'

The three girls spent the allotted time talking about what they liked to do. Mia loved Jane Austen and chess, and Hu played the violin and had four brothers. For the last fifteen minutes of class, they watched a video on debating.

The rest of the day went by fast, and after

the last bell, Ellyse checked her phone. Dad had texted back: *Good luck! See you at five.*

He probably thinks I'm on the team, she thought glumly, and trudged off to change into her training gear.

* * *

Ellyse made her way to the field, holding her bat under her arm tightly. Emma saw her first and ran over.

'What are you doing here?' she said, glancing around. 'Parkes won't be happy, you know.'

'She can make me leave training, but she can't stop me from watching,' Ellyse said.

Emma smiled. 'You're pretty tough for a little kid. Don't say we didn't warn you.'

Ellyse dumped her schoolbag and placed her bat on top. 'Are we still doing catching and throwing?'

'Yep. Come on, then.'

Without a word, the other girls added her to the drills. Nicola sent her out to the boundary and, when Ellyse was able to easily throw the ball all the way in to the wickets, she got an approving nod.

Her heart sank when Ms Parkes walked onto the pitch. 'Keep up the drills for another ten minutes, girls,' she ordered. 'I want you all aiming to improve accuracy as well as distance. Then we'll . . .' She broke off and strode across the field to Ellyse. 'What on earth are you doing here? I told you –'

'Can't I at least train with the team?' Ellyse asked.

'Absolutely not. I don't want you dragging them down.' The teacher pointed to the boundary. 'Off the field – now!'

'Yes, miss.' Ellyse walked over to her bag, her face flaming with embarrassment. For a moment, she almost gave in to tears. *No, I won't leave! I'm going to stay and watch. I don't care what she says.*

Ms Parkes glared at her a few times, but she ignored it. The way Ms Parkes ran a training session was nothing like Bob Oates at the club. Bob was great at giving everyone a turn, showing them techniques and giving them exercises for particular skills. Ms Parkes seemed to be very good at shouting and telling players they were useless.

After the throwing and catching drills, she made the girls run around the field four times until they were all puffing. Only then did she allow them to play a game. She stood behind the bowler's end like an umpire and twice, just as Nicola was about to bowl, she snapped something that made Nicola falter and almost trip.

Ten minutes later, Ms Parkes left the field and the team gathered in a huddle on the pitch.

'Want to play?' Nicola called out to Ellyse. 'Ms Parkes won't be back. She coaches a boys' team somewhere and always leaves early on a Tuesday.'

Ellyse scrambled to her feet. 'Sure! Where do you want me?' *I bet they send me out to third man.*

'How about you bat for a couple of overs?' Nicola said. 'Caitlin's a spin bowler and she needs a bit of a challenge.'

Ellyse quickly padded up and took the helmet, then set herself up at the wicket, prodding the pitch. It wasn't in very good condition, so a decent spin bowler could really make the ball move. She scanned for fielders, then concentrated on batting. Caitlin was a fairly good leg spinner with plenty on the ball but Ellyse was able to hit a few boundaries.

Before she knew it, her dad was standing on the edge of the field, watching. She'd been able to bat, bowl and do some fielding, and had had a great time. What a pity it was only for today.

'You did well out there,' her dad said on the way home. 'When's your first game?'

Ellyse swallowed, her mouth dry. 'I'm not in the team, Dad. They let me train today because Ms Parkes wasn't there.'

'Who's Ms Parkes?'

'She's the coach, and she said I can't be in the team because I'm too small.' Ellyse stared miserably out the window, hoping Dad wouldn't be upset, but of course he was.

'She can't do that!' He drummed his fingers on the steering wheel. 'I'll go and talk to someone at the school tomorrow.'

'No, don't.' Ellyse put her hand on his to stop the tapping. 'She might change her mind. The other girls might even be able to convince her to let me play. I don't want you to make it worse – please?'

'Hmmm.' Dad thought for a few moments. 'All right, I'll leave it for now, but I'm not happy about it.'

Neither am I, Ellyse thought, but didn't say anything more.

CHAPTER SIX

Ellyse was looking forward to her first PE class on Wednesday morning. As she changed into her sports uniform, she wondered whether the PE teacher would let them play cricket or tennis, or make them do gym or... Actually, it wouldn't matter. Ellyse liked lots of sports and she couldn't wait to run around instead of sitting in a chair all day.

She pulled on her polo shirt and sighed. It was the smallest size and still she could've fit two of her inside it. *Maybe Mum could take it in a bit*, she thought. The material was so new that it felt stiff and prickly.

'I hate these shorts.' Next to her, Hu stared down at the baggy green shorts that flapped around her thighs. 'They are *so* uncool.'

Ellyse's own shorts looked like a skirt. 'At least your shirt fits.'

Hu laughed. 'Watch out if it's windy. You might sail away.'

'Gee, thanks.' They followed the others out of the changing room and lined up at the gym entrance. Inside, two teams of older girls were playing a fast game of basketball.

'I hope we get to play volleyball,' said Hu. 'Or soccer.'

'You like soccer?' Ellyse grinned. 'Do you play on the –'

'Quiet!' Ms Parkes stood in the doorway, scowling. 'Even new Year Sevens should know better than to chatter like cockatoos when you're waiting for a teacher.'

Of course Ms Parkes is our PE teacher. Ellyse closed her eyes in despair. *I'm doomed.*

'Right, I want you to do three laps of the field behind the gym. No chatting, no whining. Off you go.'

Ms Parkes eyed each one of the girls as they filed past her. When she spotted Ellyse, her lips thinned.

'Hey, Ms Parkes really gave you the evil eye back there,' Hu said, as she jogged next to Ellyse. 'What'd you do to upset her?'

'I want to be in the cricket team,' Ellyse replied. 'She told me I was too small, but I went to their training session anyway.'

'Oooh.' Hu was puffing as they completed the first circuit. 'I am so unfit. You're not even breathing hard.'

'I do lots of running for cricket on Saturdays.' Ellyse looked around. 'I don't think everyone is going to make it.'

Sure enough, half of the girls walked the last lap, which made Ms Parkes grumpy. 'This is not good enough,' she barked. 'Our athletics day is in three weeks and you all have to compete in at least two events.'

A loud chorus of groans greeted this announcement.

'I'm terrible at running,' a girl complained.

'There are plenty of other events,' Ms Parkes said. 'Today we'll focus on running, hurdles, shotput and javelin.'

'What's a javelin?' someone whispered.

Ellyse knew and was burning to have a go at it.

Ms Parkes divided up the class and sent each group to a different area to practise their event. The teacher went with the javelin and shotput groups first to show them throwing techniques and told the others to do sprints in the meantime.

Ellyse and Hu followed their group to the other side of the oval, where a row of hurdles had been set up. Ellyse sat down and began her stretches.

'What are you doing?' Hu asked.

'Warming up,' Ellyse replied. 'It's easy to strain a muscle or hurt yourself otherwise.'

Hu sat on the grass and began to copy her. 'Ugh, it hurts.'

'That's your hamstring,' Ellyse said, chuckling. 'It might be better to start off more gently.'

The other girls ignored them and began measuring their legs against the wooden tops. 'I'll never get over this,' one of them said. 'I'm scared of falling on it.'

Ellyse wasn't so sure about the hurdles either. They were higher than her thighs. *Is Ms Parkes ever going to come and show us how to jump?* she thought impatiently. The running group was jogging up and down, trying to go very slowly.

When Ms Parkes finally arrived, she joined the two groups together. 'Who's done hurdling before?' she asked.

Nobody put up their hand.

'We haven't got time to go through the technique today, so you will all be running races.' Ms Parkes ignored the sighs of relief. 'Two hundred metres, in lots of four.'

Ellyse was in the first group and lined up at the start.

'Ready, set, GO!' Ms Parkes shouted, and they were off.

As she ran, Ellyse felt her shorts and shirt flapping madly around her. Hu was right – it was like being a sailing ship. Ellyse ran faster, catching up to the girl in front of her. They crossed the line together, the other girls at least ten metres behind.

Each group took a turn, Hu winning her race by several metres. 'Hey, that wasn't so bad,' she said.

While she waited, Ellyse had been watching the javelin throwers. It looked fun and sort of like fast bowling in cricket. She hoped there'd be time to try it out.

But Ms Parkes made them run again – the one hundred metres this time – and to Ellyse's dismay, after she'd won her race, Ms Parkes said, 'Karen, Hu, Ellyse, Jessica, Lisa, I've put you down for the one hundred and two hundred metres. Those will be your two events.'

Ellyse took a deep breath and put up her hand. 'Ms Parkes, can I please try the javelin?'

'Not today. Two more circuits of the oval, girls, while I sort out the other groups.' She walked across the field, leaving Ellyse open-mouthed.

This is so unfair! It wouldn't have killed her to let me try!

* * *

Ellyse was still fuming when school finished for the day, but the fact she had training that night cheered her up. When Dad took her to the cricket ground, Jamie and the others were already there, and she quickly warmed up and joined them for fielding drills. It was great to be back with her mates instead of looking nervously over her shoulder for Ms Parkes all the time.

After the drills, Bob divided them up into his usual 'shirts' and 'no shirts' teams to play a game, with Ellyse on the 'shirts' team. She always ended up in 'shirts', although it had taken her a while to work out why!

Bob put her in to bat. 'I want to see your feet moving more, Ellyse,' he said. 'Remember to get your head forward first so your weight is in the right place.'

The Hoppers' captain, Will, was bowling, which meant she had to focus one hundred per cent. Will often got the ball to turn a lot, and an edge would see her easily caught out in slips.

Bob stood off to the left and watched, calling calm instructions to everyone: 'Move in a bit, Tyler', 'You're twisting your shoulder, Will' and 'Get on to that shorter ball, Ellyse'. Then it was her turn to bowl, and she had two good overs, placing the ball well down the pitch and forcing the batsmen to mostly defend.

Bob put her at third man for fielding and she watched Jamie bat, wishing he'd hit to her. But he didn't. He knew she'd send it back too quickly or maybe catch him out. At the end of the session, Bob called them all together.

'Good training tonight, Hoppers,' he said. 'We're playing St Joe's on Saturday morning, and they're coming second on the ladder.'

'We're top, though,' Will said.

'Easy enough to get knocked off our perch,' Bob said, frowning. 'Especially if you get too cocky.' He paused. 'Perch. Cocky. Get it?'

Everyone groaned.

'All right, all right,' Bob said. 'It wasn't one of my best. All the same, I want each one of you on your toes. We want to win convincingly. We're sure to play them in the finals, so let's give them something to think about. See you here at quarter past eight sharp.'

On the way home, Ellyse ran through the session in her head. 'Can we go to the nets tomorrow after school?' she asked her dad. 'I don't think I'm moving my feet enough.'

'Sure. I know a batting drill we can do that'll help.'

'Cool.' Ellyse relaxed. Dad always seemed to know what drill would help and what skill she needed to work on. She couldn't wait to practise again, to get that feeling of hitting the ball exactly the way she wanted and seeing it zoom out to the boundary.

As for the Callinan team, she liked Nicola and the others, and playing with them was fun, but was it worth getting on Ms Parkes's bad side? *Maybe not*, Ellyse thought.

She hated giving in, but being ordered off the field like that was mega-embarrassing. Besides, worrying about it might affect her Saturday game. *The Callinan XI can survive without me*, she resolved, as they pulled up to the house.

CHAPTER SEVEN

Ellyse didn't go near the cricket field on Thursday. Instead, she sat under the trees with Charlie and Jazz.

'My class are a bunch of zombies,' Charlie said. 'Everyone is good all the time and nobody talks. It's so booooooring!'

Jazz grinned. 'That would just about kill you, Charlie, not being able to talk.'

'My class is like that too,' Ellyse said. 'Still, it's only the first week. I bet everyone will eventually loosen up and start acting like they did at primary school – talking and writing notes and being late.'

'Except we didn't get detention for that in primary school,' Jazz said, and shuddered. 'Our English teacher, Mrs Roberts, is a dragon. She told me I had to do as well as Liana. As if! Liana is a super-brain.' Liana was Jazz's older sister.

They all agreed that being in different classes was no fun at all. 'Have you made any friends in your class?' Charlie asked them.

'Sort of,' Ellyse said. She sat next to Hu in nearly every class and they talked a bit. Did that count?

'No matter what, we're still besties,' Jazz said. 'Hey, let's go to the movies on Friday night.'

Ellyse bit her lip. 'I'll have to ask, and it'd have to be early because –'

'We know,' Jazz and Charlie chorused. 'You've got cricket on Saturday morning!'

* * *

Friday night came and they met at the shopping centre and wandered around the stores, trying on clothes and looking at make-up. In one store, Jazz tried on a pair of jeans and gazed at herself in the mirror.

'I love these!' she squealed.

'They do look really cool,' Charlie said.

Ellyse checked the price tag. 'Ouch, they're two hundred dollars.'

Jazz frowned and took them off. 'Mum'll never buy these for me. She'd say it was two weeks' worth of groceries.'

'Come and check out shoes instead,' Charlie said.

Ellyse caught sight of a display of new cricket shoes on sale. 'Hey, look at these. Forty per cent off *and* they've got red studs. I want them.'

Jazz and Charlie rolled their eyes. 'Only you would want cricket shoes instead of new jeans,' Jazz said, laughing.

Charlie took out her phone and gasped. 'We're gonna miss the movie! Come on!'

They ran through the centre, weaving through shoppers and dodging prams, and made it to their seats, laughing and spilling popcorn everywhere, just as the title burst on to the screen. The movie was a scary one with an alien monster that hunted people.

'Who picked this?' Ellyse whispered. 'I thought it was meant to be a comedy.'

'Oops, I think we're in the wrong cinema,' Jazz whispered back.

'Shush,' said the man behind them.

They crept out, spilling more popcorn, and rushed next door, falling into their seats in fits of giggles. Just as well it was a comedy and they could laugh all they wanted without people going, 'Sssshhhhh!'

* * *

Ellyse was up early the next day. After getting her cricket gear ready, she headed to the kitchen and made herself a hearty breakfast.

'Leave some for your brother,' Mum said, swooping in to rescue the yoghurt container.

'Serves him right for sleeping in,' Ellyse said with a cheeky grin.

'His game's not until eleven,' Dad said, coming down the stairs. He held Ellyse's cricket hat and pulled at its twisted brim. 'What happened to this?'

Ellyse grimaced. 'I put it in the washing machine and it shrunk, but at least it fits properly now.'

Having bits of uniform that were way too big was an eternal problem. Ellyse's mum was handy at taking in shirts and shorts, but hats were different.

As the Hoppers were playing an away game, they had to drive for over half an hour to get there. The ground had no pavilion or much shade, so Ellyse's dad set about putting up the two big beach umbrellas he always carried in the boot.

Ellyse warmed up with her team, and when Will won the toss, they decided to bat first. Bob put her at number five, and she and Jamie sat near Dad, who was scoring for them.

'How's your new school?' Jamie asked.

Ellyse shrugged. 'It's good . . . big . . .'

'Are you in the cricket team yet?'

'No. The coach hates me. Told me I was too small.' She pulled up some grass, piling it on top of her cricket bat.

Jamie poked her arm. 'You need more muscles. Me and the guys are going to the gym now. You should come.'

She made a face. 'Yeah, maybe. A gym's not going to make me grow ten centimetres, though, is it?'

'A torture rack might!'

Will and Vijay were batting out in the middle, and Will was struggling against St Joe's spin bowler.

'Is he new?' Ellyse asked her dad.

'First time I've seen him,' Dad said. 'He's pretty good.'

The next ball bounced in front of Will and curved around behind his legs to hit the wickets. Will looked astounded, as if he couldn't believe it had happened. He was given out and stomped off the pitch, scowling. Jamie leapt up and made his way to the wicket.

Ellyse felt guilty. *Oops, we should've been watching the play, especially this new bowler.*

Jamie hit the next ball for a single, and put Vijay on strike. He defended well until the end of the over and then Jamie was on strike again. Will, meanwhile, was sulking on the sideline. Bob told him to pick up his bottom lip before he tripped over it.

The next St Joe's bowler was fast, with a good action and follow-through but nothing tricky other than pace. Jamie and Vijay scored a half-dozen runs off that over and the Hoppers were sitting on 1/24 after six overs. It wasn't bad, but they had a way to go yet.

Except St Joe's spin bowler had the ball again, and suddenly Vijay was out, after misjudging the spin and edging the ball into slips. On the last ball of the over, Jamie got sucked in by a slow leg spinner, came too far forward and missed. The wicketkeeper stumped him, and just like that the Hoppers were 3/24.

Ellyse sat there, stunned by their wickets falling so fast.

'You're up,' Dad said. 'You'll be fine – you'll face their pace man now. Just remember to keep your eye on that ball.'

'Yes, Dad.' She gulped down some water and headed towards the pitch, her bat under her arm as she buckled on her helmet. Her heart banged against her ribs and she took a few deep breaths to calm herself. *Focus, breathe, watch the ball.* She ignored the gleeful grins of the St Joe's team. *They might think they've got us on the ropes, but I'm not giving in that easily.*

Jamie passed her halfway and scowled. 'Sorry. That was dumb.'

'You'll make up for it when you bowl them all out,' she said.

Ben scored a single off the first ball and then Ellyse was on strike. At the wicket, she took her time checking the pitch, getting her grip right and scanning to see where the field was set. She knew this St Joe's bowler from other games and it added to her confidence when she judged his pace and line and managed to hit a boundary on the third ball. Down the other end, their number four, Ben, had an agonised look on his face, and she guessed he was praying for a single on the last ball of the over so she'd be the one facing the spin bowler.

A single from her, two from Ben and, by the conclusion of the over, she was at the batting end.

I need a strategy. Play defensive, pick my shots, don't get fooled.

Off to her left, a St Joe's player called, 'Come on, Sam, it's just a girl. Easy pickings.'

The bowler laughed and walked back for his run-in.

Just a girl? Right, I'll show them.

The bowler sent down a ball that shifted a little, but she was able to block it.

He's trying me out. The next one will be a test.

Sure enough, he put plenty of spin on it, but again she kept her eye on the ball and defended. Two more balls, two more defensive shots. The bowler didn't look so happy now; a frown creased his forehead and he tossed the ball up and down a couple of times. She knew he'd try to make his next one a killer.

Ellyse watched how it left his hand, the seam hidden until the last instant, the way it rolled in the air and seemed to pick up pace as it dropped. It was a leg spinner and it'd move away from her. She played another defensive shot, into the ground.

The St Joe's boys groaned.

Too bad, so sad. She hid a smile and got ready again.

This time the bowler was impatient; the ball was faster and had less spin on it. She watched it all the way, stepped forward and hit it hard. The ball soared past the bowler and down to the boundary. Four! That put Ben on strike for the next over.

Gradually, over by over, she and Ben kept the score ticking along, a few at a time. Mostly it was Ellyse who faced the spinner, then, as other bowlers took their turns, she was able to hit out a bit more. Ben went out on 31, and Marko came in to score 19. By the time the Hoppers finished their innings, Ellyse was on 50 and they'd scored a total of 124.

Just a girl, hey?

CHAPTER EIGHT

The Hoppers gathered around Ellyse, smacking her on the back and high-fiving each other.

'You played well,' Bob said. 'Good tactics, lots of patience. That's what I like to see.'

Ellyse smiled and ducked her head. *Wow, praise from Bob!*

'You did play well,' said someone behind her.

Ellyse turned to find a young, familiar-looking woman holding out her hand. She shook it shyly. 'Thanks.'

'I'm Maddy Dawson.' The woman's smile was wide under her shady hat. 'I'm watching a few club games today. I was going to go on to Epping but I might stay a bit longer to watch you bowl.'

'Me?' Ellyse squeaked. It had just sunk in who Maddy Dawson was. She was one of New South Wales' best cricketers and an Australian test player!

'I'm a selector now for the junior squads,' Maddy explained. 'When do you turn eleven?'

'I'm twelve,' Ellyse said, a little indignantly. 'Thirteen in November.'

'Really?' Maddy turned to Ellyse's dad. 'Are you feeding this girl enough?'

He laughed but shot Ellyse a sympathetic look. 'She'll grow when she's ready.'

'Well, she can definitely handle a bat.'

Bob called the team together for a talk before the next innings. 'It's getting hot out there, so keep up your water intake. A hundred and twenty-four isn't a huge total to chase, but we're not going to make it easy for them with silly bowling or fielding, are we?'

'No, Bob,' everyone chorused.

'Ellyse, warm up. Jamie, you bowl the first over, and keep it tight. I don't want them racking up fifteen or twenty off the very first over.' Bob clapped his hands. 'Let's get to it, Hoppers.'

'Go, Hoppers!' the team shouted.

Ellyse drank half a bottle of water, ate an orange quarter and ran onto the field. She'd be in the outfield as usual, but she was itching to bowl. She'd watched the batsmen carefully in the first over, taking in how they moved their feet and held their bats. Both of the St Joe's openers were solid players and they'd clearly been told to settle in. Still, they scored six off Jamie's bowling.

Ellyse took the ball and rubbed it on her pants, trying to put a bit of shine back on it. The players at the wickets met in the middle to mutter to each other, and one of them smirked at Ellyse. She smiled back and rubbed the ball some more.

Back at his wicket, the smirker took his time getting ready, but as soon as he looked up, she was off. A steady run-in, arm over fast and the ball sizzled down the pitch, landing at his feet and bouncing up. He was forced back, dabbing at it defensively. The ball snicked off the side of his bat and into the wicketkeeper's gloves.

'Howzat!' Ellyse cried.

The umpire's finger went up. Out!

The Hoppers ran in to slap Ellyse on the back again.

'Easy!' Ben called.

'Calm down,' Will said. 'Remember what Bob said – no need to get silly.'

Everyone nodded and tried to be serious, but an early wicket was a real advantage. They all went back to their positions and Ellyse got ready to bowl again. The new batter was the St Joe's spin bowler, and she suspected he'd be just as good with the bat. Why else would they put him in at number three? She bowled another fast ball, but it didn't have the length this time and was smacked away for a four.

Darn it!

'Bowl your own game, little one,' her dad called from the boundary.

Thanks, Dad. Like I need that reminder! But he was right. If she tried to bowl to get this one guy out, her rhythm and stride would be affected. She had to stick to what she did best and go for the yorker.

Sure enough, she was able to make him defend, and it wasn't until the fifth ball that he hit into midfield and got a run. That left the other batter to face her for one ball. He would've been watching where her balls landed, and she could tell he was expecting another one the same. So this time she went for a full toss. He managed to hit it cleanly but it went straight to the midfielder, who fumbled, grabbed and held on to it. Two out!

Ellyse looked over to the boundary and discovered Maddy Dawson had left. She tried not to feel disappointed – after all, Maddy wasn't there to pick a rep team. The big regional and interstate competitions were over for the season. *Maybe Maddy will remember me next season*, Ellyse thought, then settled in to concentrate on getting St Joe's out as soon as possible.

The game went right to the wire. In the last over, St Joe's needed eight to win with five wickets in hand. Ellyse had just bowled, and Jamie was going to take the ball. Could he keep them from scoring? It was so hot by then that they'd needed two drinks breaks. Jamie ran in, bowled a long ball and the batter had to block it. But on the next ball, he hit it and they ran. The ball kept going to the boundary. Four!

St Joe's only needed four more to win. The batter on strike was their opener. He'd managed to stay in for the whole innings and was on 79. He had to be tired. On the other hand, he knew Jamie's bowling now and was ready.

The next ball Jamie bowled was a little short, and the batter gave it a mighty whack.

The ball rose like a rocket, heading straight for Ellyse. She moved forward, eyes glued to it, waiting as it arced high and fell through the air. Right into her hands. *Smack!* Her hands stung but she held on to it.

Out!

The batters had crossed while the ball was in the air. The new batsman didn't have to face the bowler, but now Jamie was bowling to St Joe's captain. He hit a short ball and they ran fast, just avoiding a run-out. Three off two balls. Ellyse wiped the sweat off her face and adjusted her hat against the sun. Jamie got ready to bowl.

The batsman took a wild swing and connected. The ball shot up into the air, over the wicketkeeper's head and raced to the boundary.

Ellyse dropped her head and closed her eyes for a moment. Then she straightened and went to shake hands with the opposition.

Bob never yelled and screamed when they lost, but shook each player's hand and said something nice to them. 'Great catch, kiddo,' he told Ellyse. 'Knew I could rely on you.'

Ellyse felt a warm glow inside. Bob's praise was like gold. Then it was time for Mrs Bob's sausage rolls and some ice-cold cordial.

On the way home, Dad said, 'You played well today. Maddy Dawson was impressed.'

'She thinks I'm too small,' Ellyse replied gloomily.

'Actually, by the time she left she was calling you the "pocket rocket".'

'Really?' Ellyse had to smile. 'Don't tell anyone. That's all I need – a new nickname.' She already got called Tiny Tim and Mouse.

Soon the season would be over, which made her sad, except then soccer would start!

And there was touch footy too, and tennis, and Dad had promised to let her have a go at golf. Wouldn't it be great to play sport all the time like the professionals did?

CHAPTER NINE

On Monday at school, she told Charlie and Jazz all about the game. 'You have to come and watch us in the final. It's in two weeks, on Saturday.'

'Is the game in the morning?' Jazz asked. 'We're going rollerskating, and the rink's only open in the afternoon.'

Ellyse looked from Jazz to Charlie and back again, a rock forming in her stomach. 'Were you going to ask me?'

'Yeah, of course,' Charlie said hastily. 'But you usually say no.'

Ellyse frowned. 'You know I play sport on Saturdays. Can't we go on Sunday?'

Jazz shrugged. 'Saturday's the only day Carla and Sheridan can go.'

Carla and Sheridan? Who are they?

'They're girls in our classes,' Charlie explained. 'They asked us and . . .'

'Carla's mum is going to drive us all,' Jazz added.

'Oh. Okay.' Ellyse forced a smile. *I'm being left out of everything!* 'Maybe another time, then.'

'Totally!' Charlie slung an arm over Ellyse's shoulder. 'Hey, we've got electives in fifth period. I can't wait. We're going to rehearse a real play.'

Ellyse noticed the big case leaning against the wall. 'Is that your guitar, Jazz?'

'Uh-huh. I nearly drove Mum mad on the weekend with my practising.' She grinned. 'Mum actually begged me to ask you guys over to play loud music and stink up the house with nail polish. She said anything but more *plunk, plunk, plunk*.'

'Not nice!' Charlie and Ellyse chorused.

The bell rang and they went off to their homerooms. Ellyse walked up the stairs, her bag dragging on her shoulders. *Am I losing my two best friends? First it was different classes, now we don't even seem to like the same things anymore. How did life change so fast? Is it this stupid school?*

There'd be no cricket at lunchtime, so she'd make sure to spend it with Jazz and Charlie. The last thing she wanted was for them to dump her.

Ellyse trudged into the classroom and let her bag slide to the floor with a *thump*.

Debating again. Mia and Hu had their heads together, making notes and arguing with each other and laughing.

'What do you think of this?' Hu said, turning the notebook around.

Ellyse scanned their points, neatly written up in bubbles and highlighted in different colours. 'Wow, you've done all the work already.'

'Not really . . . we want your ideas too.' Hu glanced at Mia, who nodded.

'Yes, you might think of something we haven't.'

Ellyse read over the notes properly. All Hu's reasons were the kinds of things teachers would say. What could she add? 'How about: if you aren't watching TV, you have more time to play sport? And, you know, get fit.'

'Exercise? Sport?' Mia made a face. 'I can't even catch a ball properly.'

'No, that's a good idea,' Hu said. 'We'll add it to the list.'

By the end of the period, they had their speeches worked out, and the teacher announced they'd start having trial debates. Groups drew their names out of a bowl and, to Ellyse's relief, her team got the lowest number, which meant their debate wouldn't be for weeks yet.

At homeroom that morning, they'd all been reminded that the school athletics day was coming up the following week. While Ellyse wanted to practise for her events, a part of her wondered if she should even bother if Ms Parkes was running things.

'Can we do some bowling tonight?' she asked Dad on the way home.

'What about your homework?' he said. 'Don't you have some?'

'Yes.' She had lots but she'd rather play cricket.

'Homework first, then,' he said. 'The final is two weeks away. Besides –' he pointed at the dark clouds piling up over the city – 'I think we're in for a storm.'

Ellyse's tummy gave a big rumble. 'I think there's a storm in my stomach. I need food!'

After an apple and some of Mum's carrot cake, Ellyse sat down at her desk. She hadn't kept up with her homework and now she had several things due at once. Subjects at high school were so much harder than primary school, and there were so many of them. She sighed and started on her piece of writing for English.

By the time she'd finished everything, dinner was on the table and rain was pelting down outside, smashing through the trees in the garden. No cricket tonight. Ellyse sat on the couch and watched TV with her family, but the show was dumb – another reason she could add to her debate team's argument. Her mind wandered. *Why is Ms Parkes so mean? Why can't I play for Callinan?* she thought over and over again. *What if St Joe's beats us in the final? And why are Jazz and Charlie doing stuff without me?*

* * *

The rest of the week dragged. While Ellyse badly wanted to play cricket with the Callinan team, she spent lunchtimes with Jazz and Charlie, and finally met Carla and Sheridan. On Friday night, they all went to the shopping centre.

As they sat in the food court, sipping their soft drinks, Carla confessed she had a crush on a boy who worked at the pizza place.

'Just go and buy some pizza!' Charlie insisted, shaking her head.

Eventually, Charlie went with Carla to order five slices while the others watched. When they came back, Jazz said, 'When he comes over, be cool, okay? Don't laugh. Boys hate girls who screech.'

Ellyse bent over her drink. *Who says stuff like that?* she thought.

'Do you like any boys?' Sheridan asked her.

Before Ellyse could answer, Jazz jumped in. 'Ellyse plays cricket with *heaps* of boys all the time.' She nudged Ellyse. 'Including Jamie Costa.'

'Oooh,' Carla and Sheridan said.

'They think Jamie's cute,' Charlie explained. 'So do lots of other girls.'

'Jamie? Cute?' Ellyse burst out laughing.

'Do you really play cricket with him?' Sheridan asked. 'Can we come and watch?'

'Er . . .' *That would totally disrupt the final.*

'That's the day we're going rollerskating,' Charlie said. 'Another time, maybe.' She rolled her eyes at Ellyse when the others weren't looking, and whispered, 'By the time they remember, cricket season will be over.'

'Thanks,' Ellyse whispered back, and tucked into her pizza.

* * *

The next day was the Hoppers' last game against the Bears, who were the second-bottom team. Despite their ranking, Bob was adamant they take the game seriously.

'Just because you know you're in the grand final it doesn't mean you can slack off,' he reminded them.

They all played well, beating the Bears by 41 runs. As they munched on Mrs Bob's sausage rolls after the game, Ellyse couldn't help thinking back to the previous night.

'Did you know there are some girls who have a crush on you?' she asked Jamie.

Ben and Vijay overheard her and laughed. 'Yeah, Costa the Cutie. Didn't you know?' Ben teased.

Jamie's face turned bright red. 'It's not funny.'

'But how do they even know who you are?' Ellyse asked.

'It's Charlie and Jazz's fault,' he grumbled. 'I saw them outside my school and they had some girls with them.'

'Don't worry,' she said, grinning. 'I'll protect you from them.'

On the way home, Dad said, 'How do you think you bowled today?'

Ellyse thought about it. 'Okay, I guess. I took two wickets . . .'

'You could do with a bit more pace, perhaps.' Dad flicked on the indicator and drove up the freeway ramp. 'Want to try some new drills this week?'

Ellyse was intrigued. 'How about this afternoon?'

He laughed. 'I should've known you'd want to start straight away.'

At the nets, Dad focused on her left arm. 'Your bowling arm is fine,' he said, 'but you need to extend your left arm more and keep your weight forward with a good follow-through.'

Ellyse frowned. 'Aren't I doing that?'

'Your left arm is flapping around a little. We're just after a bit more control, okay?'

Training with Dad was great – he never got mad or impatient. After two hours, though, he was ready to put up his feet.

'You can practise with Jamie and the others during the week,' he said.

She definitely would. Something had changed in her bowling – something for the better – and she couldn't wait to try it out on the boys.

CHAPTER TEN

Monday came, and Ellyse had promised to meet Jazz and Charlie at lunchtime. Jazz wanted her friends to listen to her sing and play the guitar.

'It's only a lunchtime rehearsal,' she'd said, but Ellyse and Charlie could see she was busting to show them what she could do.

When the lunch bell rang, Ellyse packed

up her geography notebook and atlas and headed for her locker.

'Hey, Ellyse!' Nicola called, running to catch up to her.

'Hi. Off to practice?'

'Yeah, a lunchtime game.' Nicola fiddled with the zip on her bag. 'Do you want to play?'

Ellyse grimaced. 'Not with Ms Parkes around, thanks.'

'She's away today,' Nicola said with a grin. 'You'll be safe.'

Ellyse was about to say, 'Absolutely!' then stopped. She'd promised Jazz. 'Sorry, I can't.'

Nicola shrugged. 'Okay, no problem. We've got eleven most of the time, so –'

'No, I want to! But . . .' *Besties forever.* 'I made a promise to someone. Can I come tomorrow?'

'Maybe,' Nicola said. 'Although, if Ms Parkes is back, then . . .' She headed off and said over her shoulder, 'We'll see what happens, hey?'

Ellyse swallowed her disappointment and went to find Jazz and Charlie in the music centre. Jazz was in a small group who played the guitar and sang together.

Charlie snorted as the first notes of 'Kumbaya' started up. 'Jazz totally hated this song in primary school,' she whispered.

Before Ellyse could answer, Jazz started singing a solo. Her voice was clear and lilting, like a flute. Everyone's mouths dropped open.

'Wow, Jazz can really sing!' Ellyse whispered, shocked.

Afterwards, Jazz's face was bright pink as her friends congratulated her. 'I was *so* nervous,' she said.

'You were great,' Charlie said. 'How come you don't sing like that at home?'

'Dunno. I guess I never took it seriously.' She pointed at the music teacher. 'It makes a difference when someone thinks you're good and helps you.'

Ellyse nodded, thinking of Dad. *That's for sure!*

* * *

The next morning, Ellyse practically leapt out of bed at the possibility of being able to play cricket at Callinan. Lugging two bags to school suddenly seemed easy and she fidgeted all morning, counting down to the lunch bell. She'd told Jazz and Charlie where she was going, and waited at the field. Sure enough, Ms Parkes was away again, although nobody knew why. Ellyse hardly cared as long as it meant she could train with the team.

They bowled and batted in the nets first, Nicola watching Ellyse closely the entire time. 'You're getting a good length down the pitch. Have you changed something?' she asked.

Ellyse nodded. 'Dad and I have been doing some special training. I guess it's helping.'

'You're lucky to have someone who knows what they're doing.' Nicola bent and picked up Ellyse's cricket ball. 'He doesn't want to come and coach us, does he?'

Ellyse laughed, then noticed Nicola's worried face. 'Are you serious?'

Nicola shook her head. 'It's fine. I just think . . .' She smiled. 'Never mind what I think. Let's play.'

They went out to the middle, Ellyse following slowly. *Something's wrong, but what can I do? I'm not even in the team.* Still, she wished they'd tell her what was going on.

Nicola decided to use the spin bowlers to give the slips fielders some practice. The team's wicketkeeper, Alice, was away, so Ellyse stood in for her. It was a strange feeling, standing right behind the wickets, ready to catch or dive or leap at every single ball.

Five minutes before the bell, they raced to the gym to change back into their uniforms. Lunchtime wasn't nearly long enough but it was better than nothing.

'Do you want to come to training tonight?' Nicola asked.

'I can't this week, sorry. My team's in the grand final this Saturday and we're having an extra session tonight.'

'Grand final, eh?' Nicola nodded. 'Mind if I come and watch?'

Ellyse gasped. 'Really? I mean, sure, if you want to.' She told Nicola the place and time.

Nicola hesitated. 'I'd like you to be in our team, but... you can see what the problem is.'

Ellyse looked around the changing room. Most of the other girls were at least fifteen centimetres taller than her and she knew that's all Ms Parkes would see. 'I understand.'

Well, that was a lie. She didn't really. It was totally unfair.

CHAPTER ELEVEN

The whole team was buzzing so much that Bob had to settle them down before he talked about who would play on Saturday.

'I know you all want to be in the team,' he said, 'but this is the final and we need to put our strongest side together. Remember, every one of you has contributed to us being top of the ladder. We couldn't have done it without you coming to training and trying your best.'

Everyone was nodding, although some faces were sad, already guessing that they wouldn't be picked. Bob announced his team of eleven, and when Vijay's and Ben's names were read out, they high-fived each other. Ellyse was pretty sure she'd be picked, but she still felt a glow of pride when she heard her name.

'Twelfth man is Mitch,' Bob said. Mitch's face lit up. He was happy to be twelfth man, carrying the drinks, even if he didn't get to play. 'However,' Bob continued, 'anything can happen in four days – the flu, a twisted ankle, the bubonic plague...'

The team groaned.

'Yeah, yeah. I want everyone to train this week and support the team, and I expect you all to come on Saturday to cheer for the Hoppers. That's what being a team is about, right?'

'Right, Bob!' they shouted.

After the warm-up, they ran through fielding drills and short sprints, then played a game. When it was Ellyse's turn to bowl, Will was batting. She quickened her pace and focused on putting Dad's advice into action. It helped that she'd practised at lunchtime with the Callinan team. She was even getting a little more top spin on the ball, and Will was having trouble dealing with it. When Jamie took Will's place with the bat, Will went to field at mid-wicket.

'Remember St Joe's has a new spin bowler,' Bob called. 'I want you to watch how the bowler and the ball behave, learning how to anticipate, how to play a tricky ball.'

Ellyse bowled to Jamie, who hit it back at her along the pitch. She fielded it and went back for the next ball. This time she didn't get the length she wanted; Jamie stepped forward and hit the ball as hard as he could. It went straight towards Will at mid-wicket, above his head. He leapt for it, stretching high, and caught it. Then, as if in slow motion, Will fell awkwardly, carried backwards by the ball's speed, and landed with one leg bent under him. His scream echoed around the cricket ground and he writhed in pain on the grass.

Oh no! Ellyse's breath caught in her throat. *This is a disaster!*

Bob raced over to Will, closely followed by the rest of the team. They stood there watching in horror as Bob gently eased Will over and released his leg, but he didn't do more than that.

Ellyse's dad crouched next to Bob. 'I've called an ambulance,' he said. 'We can't move him in case we make it worse. It could be just a sprain or it could be an ACL.'

Anterior cruciate ligament injury, common in football and basketball. But cricket? It might mean a big operation. Ellyse shuddered. Will was moaning with the pain, tears sliding down the side of his face. She felt awful. *Maybe I shouldn't have bowled so hard.*

As if he were reading her mind, Bob looked around at the team. 'This is nobody's fault,' he said firmly. 'It was just bad luck that Will landed the way he did. We're all really sorry, but it was nobody's fault – not even Will's – all right?'

'Yes, Bob,' they said in subdued voices.

Training was over for the night. The team packed up and made their way off the field, leaving Ellyse and her dad to help Bob.

'I've rung Will's parents,' Dad said. 'They're on their way.'

Will was lying on his back, his face almost white. 'Does this mean I can't play on Saturday?'

Bob shook his head. 'It's not looking good, mate. Sorry.'

Will's mouth set in a hard line and he closed his eyes. Ellyse's stomach churned and she couldn't think of anything encouraging to say. The ambulance drove onto the field and two paramedics got out. They took over, listening as Bob described what had happened, then gently examined Will's leg. A few minutes later, after his parents arrived and were told the news, they loaded Will into the ambulance and drove away.

Ellyse packed up her cricket gear and trudged to the car. Her kitbag felt like it weighed ten tonnes.

Dad took it from her and put it in the back, then gave her a hug. 'Remember what Bob said, little one. It was no one's fault. These things happen.'

'I know.' She sighed. 'I just feel so bad for him. Our first grand final and he's going to miss it, isn't he?'

'I'm afraid so.'

That evening, she could hardly eat her dinner. The spaghetti looked like long white worms. When the phone rang, she nearly jumped out of her seat.

A few minutes later, Dad came back. 'Good news. It's not a full ACL, just a sprain. He'll be off it for a while and will have to use crutches. Definitely no cricket final, though.'

For the first time, instead of worrying about Will's knee and whether he'd need an operation, Ellyse realised what it would mean for the team. Not only was Will one of their best players, he was also their captain. Who would take over? Probably Jamie. But now Mitch would be in the team and Bob would have to choose another twelfth man.

Our hopes of winning the grand final are going up in smoke, she thought miserably.

The next day, she couldn't stop thinking about the batting order and who would be captain. At least the final would be a home game. Maybe Will would come and watch. But that would be awful for him since he couldn't play. She got told off three times in class for daydreaming, and eventually had to push it out of her mind and concentrate on her schoolwork.

Charlie and Jazz were sympathetic. 'Do you think you can still win?' Jazz asked.

'Maybe,' Ellyse said. 'All we can do is try.'

But it seemed impossible.

CHAPTER TWELVE

On Thursday morning, as she was walking through the school gates, someone tapped her on the shoulder. It was Nicola. 'Hey. Can you come to training at lunchtime?'

Hmm, Dad said not to overdo it but...
'Okay.'

Nicola grinned. 'We might have a surprise for you.'

If Ms Parkes was still away, maybe they wanted her to play with them in a match. But there didn't seem to be any point. Besides, the final on Saturday was much more important.

When the lunch bell rang, she ate with Jazz and Charlie. Carla and Sheridan were also there, and all they talked about was going rollerskating.

'It's, like, so loud in there,' Carla said. 'There's coloured lights and they have games and prizes too.'

'They're talking about having a roller derby competition,' Sheridan said. 'My big sister wants to be in that. It's *amazing*. They make up names for themselves, like Killercat and Betty Sock 'Em and Zooming Lucy.'

'Don't you have to be really tough and knock people over?' Jazz asked.

'Well, yeah,' Sheridan said, 'but she said

that's half the fun.'

'It wouldn't be if you got badly hurt, though,' Charlie said.

Sheridan sniffed. 'That only happens to wusses.'

There was a prickly silence, and Ellyse checked her watch. 'I have to go, sorry.' She leapt up, glad to get away. 'Have a great time on Saturday.'

'Good luck with the final,' Charlie said.

'Say hello to Jamie from me,' Sheridan added.

'Um, sure.' Ellyse escaped and found herself worrying about Will again. *At least Bob will sort things out tonight*, she thought. When she reached the field, she was surprised to see the whole team there, and counted eleven girls. *What? They don't need me at all.*

Nicola turned and waved at Ellyse. 'Over here!'

As she got closer, the girls moved back and Ellyse was met with a familiar face. Maddy Dawson grinned at her. 'Hiya, Pocket Rocket.'

Ellyse gaped. 'What are you doing here?' *Oops, that sounds a bit rude.* 'I mean, hi.'

'Maddy's our new coach!' Nicola said, unable to stop beaming. 'Ms Parkes was headhunted by another school. She's gone to "pull them up by their bootlaces".'

'Lucky them,' someone murmured.

'That's awesome,' Ellyse said. 'Are you a PE teacher, too?'

'No, I'm just here for the cricket,' Maddy said. 'I hear you might be keen on joining Callinan's First XI.'

'Totally! But . . .'

Maddy raised her eyebrows.

'Ms Parkes said I was too small. I'm only in Year Seven, and everyone else is up here.' Ellyse lifted her hand way above her head.

'I've seen you play,' Maddy said. 'I don't think you'll have any trouble keeping up with these girls.'

Ellyse looked around, half-expecting to see some scowls, but even Emma looked happy. *I can't believe it – I'm in the Callinan team!*

'We have a game tonight, but I know you're training for Saturday's final,' Maddy said. 'We're coming to cheer you on.'

'You are?' Ellyse's mouth suddenly went bone-dry. The final had turned into a big black pit and she was falling in fast. *No Will, no team captain and now Maddy Dawson and the entire Callinan team are coming.* Ellyse gulped. *What if I play terribly and let everyone down?*

Ellyse raced to training that night, dying to hear what Bob's game strategy was going to be. Usually, he talked about motivation, discipline and concentration. He was always strict about sportsmanship and hated sledging. Anyone who mouthed off missed out on Mrs Bob's sausage rolls after the game. But this was the grand final! Surely he'd have special training set up.

Instead, the whole team spent time in the nets, did some fielding and catching practice and then Bob told them to sit down. They formed a semicircle around him.

'Obviously, Mitch is now in the team,' he began. 'I've had a good think about it and I've chosen Ammar for twelfth man.'

Ammar looked gobsmacked. He barely managed to croak a thank-you.

Bob looked around at the team. 'That leaves the captaincy. It's not an easy job. You're setting the field, managing your players, keeping up morale, making sure everyone stays focused. It can affect your own play if you're not careful.' He paused and everyone held their breath. 'So I've chosen Ellyse.'

Ellyse was stunned. 'Me? What about Jamie? He'd be much better than me.'

'No, I wouldn't,' Jamie said, punching her on the arm. 'You'll be a great captain.'

'But . . .' She looked around at the other Hoppers. They were all cheering and clapping and, behind them, Dad gave her the thumbs up. She grinned back at him. *Captain!*

* * *

Ellyse was buzzing all the way home. She ran through the house and found her mum reading on the back deck.

'That's fantastic!' Mum said. 'Well done.'

It was only at dinner that Ellyse remembered to tell them about Maddy Dawson and the Callinan team.

'It's been quite a day, then,' Dad said. 'You'll be too excited to sleep.'

She did lie awake for a while, thinking about how quickly everything had changed. Even high school was starting to feel more real and not quite so big. She knew her teachers a bit better now and had some new friends as well as her old ones.

Then it was morning, the sun streaming through the gap in her curtains, and she was off to school for the athletics day.

Her two races were over early and she came second in both; only then could she relax and watch everyone else. Hu won her 400 metres heat and made it into the final; Jazz and Charlie were both competing on the other side of the field in long jump and Ellyse couldn't see them. Lots of girls fell during the hurdles races and Ellyse winced every time someone hit the ground – it reminded her of Will falling and the way his leg had twisted under him.

Nicola and Emma were helping with the judging and timekeeping. Ellyse asked about the cricket game, but Nicola made a face and said they'd lost by four wickets. 'But we'll have you in the team next week, won't we?'

'For sure,' she replied.

She spotted Hu lining up for her final and ran over to watch. The competitors all looked so much bigger, but when the starter's gun popped, Hu ran like the wind, her short legs pumping hard. Ellyse jumped up and down, cheering, 'Go, Hu! Go, Hu!'

And Hu won — by a nose! She leaned forward at the line and crossed first.

Wow, Ellyse thought, *that doubly proves it. You don't have to be the biggest at all!*

CHAPTER THIRTEEN

Saturday morning, and Ellyse was up early, although the game wasn't until one o'clock. She spent the morning fidgeting, checking and re-checking her gear. Even the 'Go get them!' texts from Jazz and Charlie didn't settle her nerves. Nothing on TV interested her and she ended up watching lots of YouTube videos of great cricket catches and top bowling.

Finally it was time to leave. Mum was coming to watch, so Ellyse sat in the back seat, trying not to bite her nails. When they got to the ground, she eagerly pushed open her door.

'Hang on,' Dad said, before she could jump out.

Ellyse waited, trying to be patient.

'I know this is a big day, love, and it's your first time as captain.' He paused and glanced at her mum, who nodded. 'Just remember that you're not playing for sheep stations. It's important but there'll be many more games and probably more finals. We just want you to have a great time and enjoy it.'

'Okay, Dad, I hear you.' And she did. His words had helped to calm the frogs leaping around in her stomach. *Play your best, that's all you need to do*, she told herself.

'Ignore all the people shouting,' Bob said

after their warm-up. 'St Joe's parents always get het up. Play with your team and for your team. Ellyse?'

'Er . . .' It was time for her first captain's talk. She'd been so busy thinking about the batting order and bowlers that she'd forgotten this bit. 'We can do this. We know their bowlers, we know they think they're better than us. We're going to prove them wrong. Go, Hoppers!'

'Go, Hoppers!' the team shouted.

Jamie was opening batsman with Vijay, who'd moved up to take Will's place. As he checked his pads and gloves, Jamie glanced at the St Joe's team setting their field. 'Who's that?' he said.

Ellyse peered across at the opening bowler. 'No idea.'

Bob frowned. It was against the rules to bring someone new into the team for the final. 'I'll check. Out you go, Jamie. Take it easy until you can judge his line and length.'

Ellyse watched anxiously as the new St Joe's player paced out his run-up and confidently moved his field around. Who was he? If he was an illegal player, Bob would sort it out.

Bob came back, shaking his head. 'They say they can prove he's played the minimum games.'

Ellyse thought it was probably someone who went to a boarding school and only played club games when he was home, which meant he could be really good. She held her breath as the boy started his run-in. He had a lot of pace and his arm coming over was a blur, the ball almost a bouncer. He meant business.

Vijay tipped the ball, sending it way over the wicketkeeper's head and down to the boundary for four. It was a great start, but Vijay didn't look happy. The next ball was just as fast, landing almost at his feet. It was all he could do to block it. It was the same for every ball after that, and the over ended with four on the board.

Now it was Jamie's turn to face their spin bowler, the one who'd got both Vijay and Jamie out in the last game. Jamie was playing safe, probably remembering how he'd been stumped last time, but Ellyse thought if he didn't attack a bit more, he'd be LBW before he knew it.

Watching was agony. She kept wanting to run out onto the pitch and tell them what to do. *Is this what being captain is like?* she wondered. *Nearly bursting with everything you want to yell at your team?*

A few seconds later, Jamie managed to score a run, which put him on strike for the next over against the unknown player. This guy seemed more confident than ever and kept moving his field around.

Ellyse watched the game on tenterhooks, riding every ball. *He's trying to psych out our batsmen.*

Jamie and Vijay were both playing defensively, Vijay getting more and more flustered by the change between pace and spin. She wanted to call out, 'Take a moment. Calm down. Breathe!' but she couldn't. When St Joe's changed bowlers to another spinner, Vijay was out LBW on the first ball.

The St Joe's parents were shouting and cheering loudly at everything. Ben glared at them as he walked to the wicket, but he had to switch focus immediately to the ball lobbing down the pitch towards him. He managed a single, putting Jamie on strike;

Jamie hit a four and then a single, so he'd face the new pace bowler.

A well-played single, and now Ben was facing. The first ball was straight and he blocked, the second swung in and went between his bat and pad, knocking his wicket over. Two out.

Fraser, in at number four, checked his pads and prepared to walk onto the field, his face pale.

'Take a few deep breaths,' Ellyse told him, 'and make them wait until you're ready. Don't let them rush you.'

He nodded, his expression grim, and set off for the middle.

Maybe I should have batted at number four, she thought. *Too late now*. She folded her arms and tried to send Fraser some good vibes. He blocked two balls, played one into the ground and the next one caught an edge and went into the keeper's gloves.

Five overs, and Hoppers were 3/13. Jamie was still in but it was a terrible start.

CHAPTER FOURTEEN

Ellyse picked up her bat and gloves, her heart crashing around in her chest. As she walked onto the field, pulling on her gloves, she passed Fraser coming off.

'Good try,' she said.

He shook his head. 'I was terrible. You're gonna have to save us – again.'

That's not what I wanted to hear. She wanted the team to pull together and win together. She met Jamie in the middle of the pitch and put her other glove on while he talked.

'They're really cocky now,' he said. 'We need to dig in for a while, stabilise things.'

'Is that new guy as tricky as he looks?'

'Nah, he's fast but he's got hardly any movement on the ball. You just have to keep your eye on it the whole time.'

'We can do this,' she said.

'Yeah, we can.' He grinned and bumped gloves with her.

Jamie was on strike, and it was St Joe's second spinner again. Jamie blocked twice and then hit a solid four. Two more defensive shots, and the sixth over was finished. Ellyse would be on strike and she waited to see who they'd put in to bowl. It was another medium-pace bowler she'd faced before.

So they're saving the really fast guy for later. Jamie had said to dig in, but they needed runs too, or St Joe's would have a piddly total to chase. She could dig in *and* belt any wayward balls. Endurance – and a bit of daring – was going to win this.

Over by over, she and Jamie added to their run total – a single here, two there and every now and then a good four. She could see St Joe's getting frustrated, and their wicket-keeper had a big mouth. He started muttering at her, just loud enough for her to hear but no one else, especially not the square-leg umpire.

'Hey, Barbie, did you bring your dolls to play with?' he snickered. 'Want to have a wussy break?' And after a bouncer skimmed her shoulder, he said, 'Aw, you'd better go and have a little cry now.'

Bob's rule was to ignore all jibes, so Ellyse decided to do exactly that. As she blocked out his voice, her focus sharpened and all she saw was the bowler, the ball and the pitch. The ball seemed slower and bigger and so easy to see – and to hit. She was playing off the middle of her bat, clean and hard, and scored two fours in a row. The last ball of the over looked like a football. She stepped forward and smacked it as hard as she could. Six!

The runs ticked along, increasing steadily, and then it was the second-last over. The really good spin bowler had been in with no effect, so now the new fast bowler returned and Ellyse was on strike.

The speed of his bowling took her by surprise. The ball zoomed towards her, landing almost at her feet, and she'd already committed to playing it. It caught an edge, rose into the air and into the hands of the fielder at first slip. The whole St Joe's team went up cheering.

I'm out! Ellyse felt like screaming.

'No ball,' called the umpire at the bowler's end.

Phew! Saved.

The bowler opened his mouth to protest and then shut it again. He stalked back for his run-in, and when he turned, he looked furious.

Your mistake, mate. This time she was ready, and played the ball straight back down the wicket, past him and out to the boundary for a four. By the end of the innings, she was satisfied that she and Jamie had done their very best. When they reached their team, the water and oranges tasted better than ever.

'That was a top captain's knock,' Bob said.

'How many did I score?' Ellyse asked. She hadn't even looked at the scoreboard.

'Sixty-four. You and Jamie managed a one-hundred-and-six-run partnership.'

Sixty-four! That's my highest ever! She couldn't hold back a beaming smile.

St Joe's target was 120. That'd be a challenge, but she knew St Joe's were up for it. She glanced at the small grandstand behind her and there were Nicola, Emma and Maddy Dawson. They all gave her the thumbs up. 'Well played,' Maddy mouthed.

Ellyse let out a huge breath. But there was no time to stress out about them watching. There was a game to win.

CHAPTER FIFTEEN

St Joe's started their batting slowly, clearly wanting to build a steady total rather than go for big hitting early. Bob suggested she have Jamie and Fraser bowl three overs each, then start changing things around, depending on how St Joe's were batting. It was good advice, and after six overs, St Joe's were on 20.

Ellyse put Vijay in to bowl next. This was where they really missed Will. He was a good leg spinner and usually took at least a couple of wickets each game. Vijay was nervous and wobbly, and the St Joe's batters took 14 off his over. Another one like that and the Hoppers would be in trouble. It was her turn to bowl and they needed a wicket.

Her first ball was a bit short, and they scored an easy single, but her second ball landed right where she wanted it. Dad's coaching was paying off big-time. The batter dabbed at it, got a slight edge and the keeper did the rest. Their first wicket. Ellyse sighed with relief.

'They're going to start attacking now,' she told her team. 'We need to stay on our toes, run down every ball and not give them time to grab anything extra.'

She turned and discovered the next batsman was the new guy. An unknown quantity.

It doesn't matter. Rhythm, line and length — that's my goal, she reminded herself.

He defended her first ball, nodded to himself and then hit the second one for two. He was good — very good. Measured and strong. He only scored one more run that over, which put him on strike for the next.

By rights, Vijay was due to bowl again, but Ellyse was considering Mitch. She'd seen him bowling in the nets at training, and Bob had been doing a lot of work with him. He batted at number ten or eleven when he played, but more importantly, he was a finger spinner and his balls were often hard to predict. She hesitated, then called him over.

'You're going to bowl,' she said.

'Me?' He looked terrified.

'Pretend you're bowling to Bob. Don't look at the batsman. Look at the pitch and where you want to put the ball, like Bob tells you. You can do this. You'll be great.'

She moved the field around, putting Jamie at silly mid-off. If Mitch could get the ball going like he did at training, they'd need fielders close in and three in slips. She went out to extra cover and waited.

Mitch's first ball went past the batsman to leg side and into the keeper's gloves. It had very little spin on it. Ellyse sucked in a shaky breath. Maybe Mitch couldn't pull this off. But the next ball had plenty of spin, like it had a mind of its own. It got past the bat and whacked into the batter's pad. Jamie and the keeper went up. 'Howzat!'

The umpire's finger rose in the air. Out! Mr Unknown was gone.

Ellyse ran in to slap Mitch on the back. 'Great bowling,' she said. 'Keep it going.'

The new batsman was the St Joe's keeper, and as he walked past her, she almost said something but bit it back. *No sledging. We're better than that.*

Mitch was muttering to himself as he walked back, and the umpire at the wicket smiled. A short run-up, a confident delivery, the ball hit the wicket and the bails flew to the ground.

Out!

'Well bowled, Mitch,' she called. 'Keep it going.' But in her head, the word *hat-trick* chimed like a bell. Would he? Could he? The new batsman was the good spin bowler – he'd probably manage spin without too much trouble.

Mitch paused at the start of his run-up and she could see his lips moving. Then he was off; the ball left his hand, curled through the air and dropped. It hit the pitch, seemed almost to stop, then suddenly moved from off to leg. The batsman hit it and looked surprised that he'd even touched it. The ball rose into the air.

Mitch put up his hands – and caught it! His mouth opened in an 'O', and it remained that way when the entire team ran in and hugged and jumped all over him.

It was the Hoppers' first hat-trick ever, and it knocked the stuffing out of the St Joe's team. The rest of their batters went down in a heap. Ellyse got three wickets, Jamie three and Vijay took the last.

After shaking hands with St Joe's players, the Hoppers lined up to be given their medals, and Ellyse was presented with the big silver cup. They did the Hoppers' cheer ten times, then they were ready to celebrate. There were none of Mrs Bob's sausage rolls today. It was a barbecue at Bob's house and, best of all, Bob had a pool.

Ellyse lay on the pink inflatable donut and dangled her legs in the cool water, smiling to herself. She kept replaying the moment Maddy Dawson had shaken her hand after the game and said, 'Can't wait to see you in the Callinan team, Ellyse. I reckon you'll be a good bet for the New South Wales team next season.'

It was going to be amazing! But it was more than six months before the next season. And in between? Soccer! Bring it on!

ELLYSE PERRY

MY WORLD

THE FACTS

FULL NAME: Ellyse Alexandra Perry

NICKNAME: Pez

BORN: 3 November 1990 in Wahroonga, NSW

HEIGHT: 176 cm

CRICKET POSITION: All-rounder; right-hand bat, right-arm medium-fast bowler

CRICKET TEAMS: Southern Stars, NSW Breakers, Sydney Sixers, Loughborough Lightning

SOCCER POSITION: Defender

SOCCER TEAM: Sydney FC

Q & A

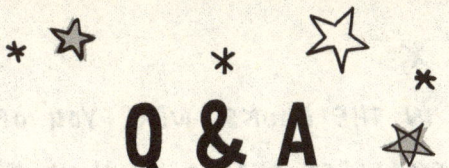

1. WHERE DID YOU GROW UP?

I grew up on the North Shore of Sydney and went to high school at Pymble Ladies' College.

2. WHAT SPORTS DID YOU PLAY AS A KID?

I liked to try different sports, although the ones I spent most of my time playing were soccer, cricket, touch football, tennis and athletics.

3. DO YOU PREFER BATTING OR BOWLING IN CRICKET?

Earlier in my career I would have said bowling, but now it's equal as I try to do both as much as I can!

4. LIKE IN THE BOOKS, WERE YOU OFTEN THE SMALLEST PLAYER IN YOUR TEAMS?

In my younger years, I was definitely on the smaller side. Whenever I was in one of the teams with the boys I was always the smallest.

5. WERE THERE ANY ATHLETES YOU LOOKED UP TO?

The main idol of mine was always Susie O'Neill – the way she carried herself at all times was so impressive. I found her to be a great model for all athletes, especially young girls.

OUT NOW

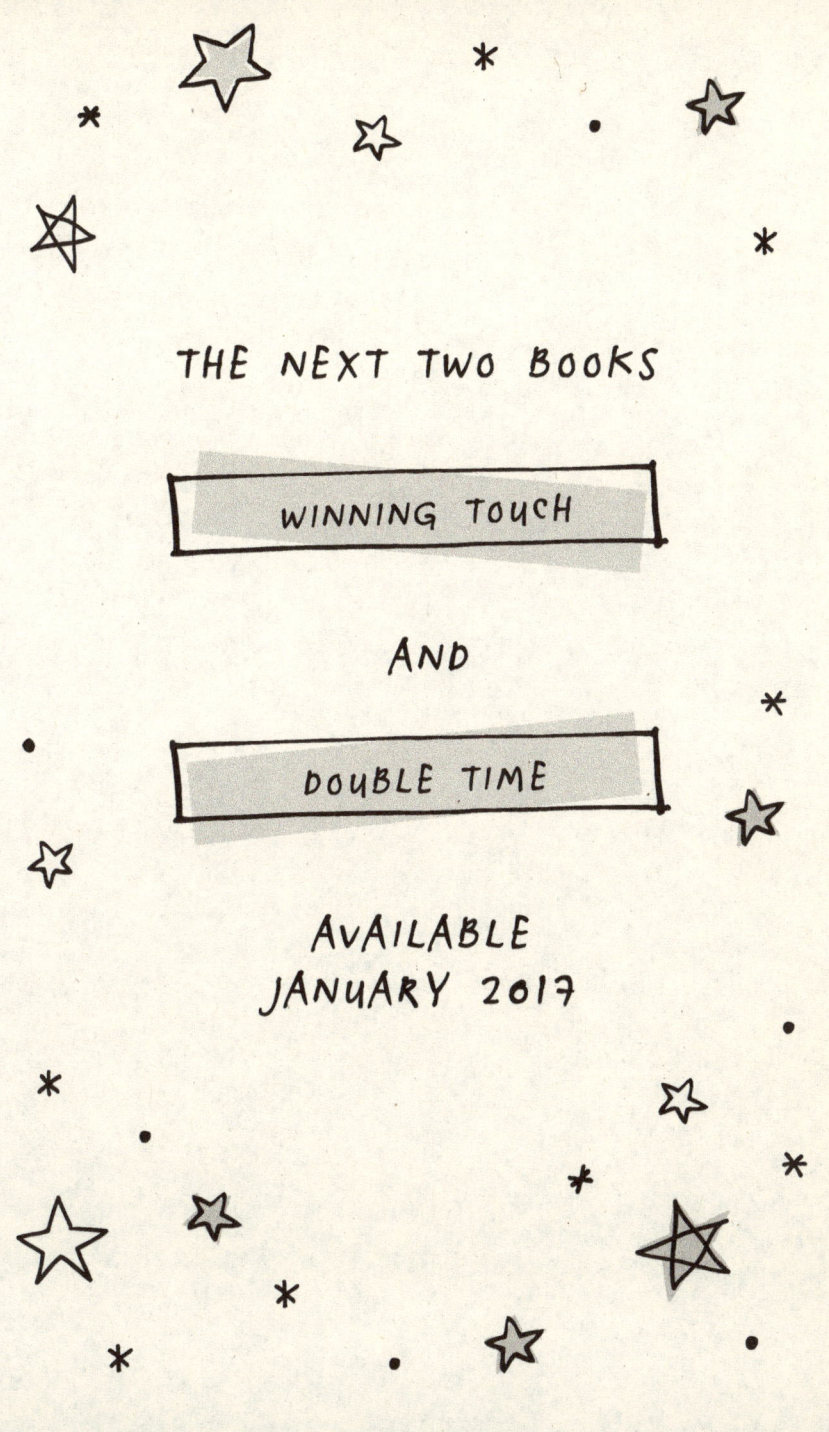

THE NEXT TWO BOOKS

Wrapping Paper

AND

Holiday Hope

AVAILABLE
JANUARY 2013